STUPID STORIES

FOR

TOUGH TIMES

Handwritten inscription:

To John

These [handwritten]

Stupid Stories

for

Tough Times

From one Crook to another [handwritten]

ANDREW CROWTHER

Best wishes [handwritten]

Andrew [handwritten]

3 Aug 2024 [handwritten]

Buxton [handwritten]

RENARD PRESS

RENARD PRESS LTD

124 City Road
London EC1V 2NX
United Kingdom
info@renardpress.com
020 8050 2928

www.renardpress.com

Stupid Stories for Tough Times first published by Renard Press Ltd in 2024

Text © Andrew Crowther, 2024

Cover design by Will Dady

Printed and bound in the UK on carbon-balanced papers by CMP Books

ISBN: 978-1-80447-111-1

9 8 7 6 5 4 3 2 1

CLIMATE POSITIVE Renard Press is proud to be a climate positive publisher, removing more carbon from the air than we emit and planting a small forest. For more information see renardpress.com/eco.

CONTENTS

TO BEGIN WITH

By and large, these stories require no introduction – or, at least, nothing I say at this point is likely to make their meaning any clearer. However, I do want to say something about 'The Light Brigade (Re-Charged)'. Most of the words are taken directly from Tennyson's original poem – but with a number of adjustments and additions. My intention is not as facetious as it may seem. I put this version of the poem together in 2018, in the aftermath of the Brexit referendum, while the British Government was in manic negotiation with itself regarding the nature of any prospective deal with the EU. In those times, I – like many others, no doubt – found the lines of 'The Charge of the Light Brigade' thundering unbidden round my head. 'Someone had blunder'd' seemed the refrain of the age. However, as I reread Tennyson's poem, I found myself dissatisfied with his romanticising of certain aspects of the incident. Despite the grotesque blunder at its heart, he seemed almost to be celebrating its folly. I don't pretend my 'corrections' are an artistic improvement, but I felt impelled to make them anyway. Mine not to reason why... This uneasy hybrid poem may seem out of place amongst the stories, but its intent harmonises with certain others, such as 'Jasper', a story I wrote in some anger during the period when Boris Johnson was Foreign Secretary. Thankfully, most of the other stories sprang from less bitter soil.

ANDREW CROWTHER

STUPID STORIES

FOR

TOUGH TIMES

THE KING'S

JUGGLER

HERE WAS A JUGGLER in the village and her name was An.

Juggling had been her passion from her earliest youth. She had seen it done when the players came to the village, and she had realised at once that it was the thing she wanted to do. She found in it a kind of freedom; it allowed her to express what was in her in a way that nothing else did.

She decided, having come of age, to make it her profession.

When the players next came to the village, she asked about joining them. The leader of the troupe was too busy to meet her and discuss the matter, naturally, but one of their administrators kindly agreed to do so.

'We're in no need of jugglers at this time,' the Administrator said.

'Oh,' said An.

'But I'll tell you what. We are very keen to encourage diversity in the arts. It is so important. I hear that the King needs a new juggler. Why don't you go in for it?'

'Thank you so much,' said An humbly. 'How do I apply?'

'Oh, I can't tell you that. I'm just tipping you the wink, you know.'

'I'm ever so grateful,' said An.

'Don't mention it. Now, where would a person get a decent cup of coffee round here?'

Having taken her leave of the Administrator, An asked around, hoping to discover how to put herself forward for the vacant post of King's Juggler. The best guess of her friends was that she would probably have to go the Palace, where her application would be considered, they imagined.

And so she set out.

At the first village she came to, she sought lodgings at the inn, and she told the landlady about her quest.

'Oh, do you juggle?' said the landlady. 'It must be lovely to be creative.'

'Oh, well, you know,' said An, blushing.

'Tell you what,' said the landlady. 'The Burgher's always on the lookout for jugglers. Why don't you try him?'

'Well, I'm off to see the King,' said An doubtfully.

'Yes, but there's no sense passing up opportunities on the way, is there?'

'No,' said An.

'I mean, no offence, but you might not get to be the King's juggler.'

'No,' said An.

'You'd have to be awfully good, and there's bound to be a lot of competition.'

'Yes.'

'And then where would you be?'

'You're quite right. I should apply to the Burgher.'

So the next morning An went round to the Burgher's house, where she found him finishing his breakfast.

'Excuse me, sir,' said An.

'Well?' said the Burgher.

'I'm sorry to be a nuisance,' said An, 'but are you looking for a juggler?'

'Could be,' the Burgher grunted.

'Would you…' said An, 'would you consider me?'

He thought for a moment. 'What can you do?' he asked.

An took her materials out of her bag and prepared herself. She took up her stand and she started to juggle the three balls. She showed him the basic moves at first, and then, as the rhythm built up, she varied it, one ball going higher than the others, so that the sequences changed and the rhythms altered, then she held a ball back and threw it with the next, then what was the same became different and what was different made its own pattern, and movement became music, which swelled and rolled following its own logic, building like a fugue until the balls themselves became an irrelevance, mere markers of the exquisite design she had woven in time and movement and then, without fuss, dismantled once more as the three balls returned to her hands and stayed there.

She bowed and waited for the Burgher's applause.

His face bore no expression at all, and he had not moved one muscle throughout the whole performance. Even his unblinking eyes gave no clue to his response. Now it was over, but he did not move for an age, until in a moment he stood up and silently left the room.

An waited, but no one came. She finally turned and left the house, hot and humiliated. Outside, a man was standing, chewing a straw.

'Are you all right?' he asked. 'I'm the Burgher's Secretary.'

An told him what had happened.

'It's all quite in order,' said the Burgher's Secretary. 'Naturally you wouldn't expect an important man like the Burgher to come to a decision just like that. The Burgher has many calls upon his time. Everything has to be done in the proper sequence, you know. You need to wait your turn like everyone else. You can't think he would make a special case for an ordinary person like you.'

'No,' said An.

'I would give him three months. That's about the optimum turnaround time. If you are unsuccessful you will not be contacted. No feedback will be given and no correspondence will be entered into. The Burgher's decision is final. Good day to you.'

'Good day,' said An.

At the next village that An stayed in, things were different. She was heartened to see that the Arts were fully organised there under a man called Gaz. He wore a leather jacket with a white vest and a chain round his neck, and anyone could see from the way he held his body that he was a man to be reckoned with.

Gaz kindly consented to watch An juggle and even to give her some feedback.

Once An had completed her performance, which wove for him a symphony in movement, he made a little sound at the back of his throat and smiled.

'First of all,' he said, 'that's really good for a beginner. Really. I mean it. There were some nice little touches. Now. You did want feedback, didn't you?'

'Yes,' said An.

'Not enough balls.'

'Sorry?'

'You haven't got anything like enough balls there, love,' said Gaz. 'You need at least five or six to keep the audience's attention. There were bits in the middle I found my attention drifting. You want to be watching that. Or hatchets. I'd watch you juggling hatchets. The stakes just aren't high enough. See what I mean?'

An said she saw what he meant.

'Then it's too short. It's all right as far as it goes, don't get me wrong, but it's nowhere near long enough for a real performance. Short form's simply not marketable. Who's going to turn up just for three minutes? It doesn't make economic sense.'

'But,' An ventured, 'this is all I've got.'

'Well, there's your problem right there, isn't it? Give us more, darling, more of everything. Longer, bigger, pizzazzier. With more balls.'

When An left the village the following morning, her step was slower and more dragging. The Palace was in her sight, high on the far hill. She would be there before the morning was through. But her heart was heavy. It scarcely seemed worthwhile continuing. After all, what had she to offer the King? Three minutes of simple juggling with three balls. No one would bother even to glance at such stuff when there were others who could juggle four, five, six balls, or cleavers, or hatchets, and not just for a few minutes but for hours on end. The whole thing was useless.

And yet, despite all this, she continued trudging along the winding road to the Palace, knowing she could not turn back, because underneath all her timidity and unsureness there was an immutable core of her being which could not be destroyed or diverted and which told her to stay firm to her resolve and to continue on her course.

She arrived at the Palace gate and a guard asked her business there.

'I am here to juggle for the King,' she said.

'I don't know about that,' said the guard, scratching his chin. 'No one's said nothing to me about no jugglers.'

'Well, could you ask?' said An, and she blushed at her boldness.

'All right then,' said the guard. 'Stay here.'

There was a long wait before he came back. There was another man with him.

'It seems it's all right,' said the guard.

'Come with me,' the man said. 'Sorry about that,' he went on, leading her down a wide corridor through the Palace. 'I am the King's Chamberlain. The fact is we haven't had as much uptake on the juggling opportunity as we expected.'

'Oh dear,' said An. 'Where did you advertise?'

'I'm sorry?' said the Chamberlain.

'I mean, who did you tell?'

The Chamberlain looked at her coldly. 'One does not tell people about these things. It is their responsibility to find out. Ah, here we are.'

They were standing in front of large, ornate double doors with gold-leaf decorations and shiny handles. An caught her breath and felt suddenly as if there were not enough air.

'Is this…? Is the King…? Is he really…?' she asked.

'Oh, yes,' said the Chamberlain. 'He's waiting for you. Well, are you ready?'

An took a moment to check her bag of tricks, then straightened her jacket, smoothed her hair, drew breath and said quietly, 'Yes.'

As if by magic, the doors opened and An stepped through into the large, dreamlike Throne Room, at the end of which sat the King in his full regalia, as he ever was and ever will be. An walked endlessly across the expanse of space. She found herself all at once in front of the throne, the King looking at her incuriously but with a solemn unblinking gaze which she tried to avoid.

An curtsied, then she set down her bag, found the three balls, croaked, 'If it please your Majesty,' and started to juggle.

She did not know at first what she was doing. Her entire being, except the automatic part which kept the balls in the air, was quite paralysed. Then she came to herself and concentrated. This was her chance. She varied the sequences, changed the rhythms, held and threw, put all she knew into every moment. Something started to emerge like a bloom, and she tended it until it flowered in an instant such as she had never known. Even as the balls flew, she smiled and almost laughed. She allowed her movements to become looser and freer, and her sense of enjoyment was visible in her performance. She broke through into a level of perfection that even she had never realised, and held it without fear until, knowing exactly the right moment to end, she ended.

And as she stood there, the performance over, she raised her head and looked at the King, and she saw he was standing and applauding wildly, an ovation all by himself, his eyes gleaming and his face split with a most wide grin.

'Yes! Yes!' he cried. 'This is she! This is my juggler!'

A moment later, it seemed, she was standing outside in the corridor again, and the Chamberlain was shaking her hand and congratulating her.

'Well done!' he said. 'Very well done indeed! May I be the first to congratulate the King's new Juggler.'

'Thank you,' said An, dazed.

The Chamberlain was guiding her away now, and explaining her duties. Banquets, feasts, ceremonial levees, private audiences…

all these things, about which he told her in great detail, went over her reeling head.

'Do I... er...' she said at last. 'Do I live in?'

'Hmm? Oh, no, we are quite a modern set-up here. You will commute in the normal manner.'

'Oh, er, good. So as to the salary?'

'Salary?'

'You know – the, er... the money?'

'Money?'

An stopped, embarrassed, as she saw the honest incomprehension in the Chamberlain's eyes.

'Yes,' she said, summoning that final deep reserve which had brought her this far. 'What do I get paid?'

'You're an artist,' said the Chamberlain. 'You do it for the honour and, of course, the exposure. Follow me – I'm sure I've seen a cupboard round here that you can change in.' He paused and looked at her. 'That is all right, isn't it?'

'Yes,' said An.

THE LAST FLING

OF ALL

N THOSE LAST MINUTES, as the missiles soared and dropped, the great leaders returned to their deep bunkers.

In every part of the world, every person, every soul, felt one searing moment of pain, as flesh stripped away.

In the silence that then fell, each person looked down at a bony arm or leg, clean and lithe and tough, and each person, now burned free of stomach, brain, heart and sex, of all the appetites that make a mortal, felt light and free.

Testing first one leg and then the other, and feeling their new lightness, they grinned with bony skulls and began, slow at first, to dance.

There remained in them no hunger or weariness, no greed, no need to slave, no earthly burden. Without breath or heartbeat, to them even time meant nothing. They danced without ceasing, each movement a joy and a celebration. They danced to music that was not heard in the ears but, like all the best music, felt inside their heads.

In time, the clouds passed; and the great leaders, aged and bowed, emerged from their bunkers, and were greeted with the sight of such grooving and jiving and revelry as had never been known.

As one, the great leaders frowned deeply and tapped a foot without speaking.

And the dead, abashed at their foolish behaviour, stopped dancing — first those nearest to the bunkers and then, in a wave, those further and further off.

They bowed their heads in shame and, one by one, they returned to their work.

BAD FREDDIE

O BEGIN WITH, Freddie was just someone who came to the office to be petted and fussed over. Freddie was a small black-and-tan dachshund, nominally belonging to Boss Sally, but in fact shared democratically among the staff.

The trouble began when some bright spark joked that Freddie should have an official role. Then some other genius came up with the title 'Interdepartmental Liaison Officer'. At first it was nothing more than a funny line; but then Freddie was given an employee badge that clipped on to his collar.

How it happened that Freddie got his own workstation, complete with PC and chair, I can't quite recall now. All I know for certain is there came a time of staff shortage when, without anyone noticing, Freddie gained a workload. He sat at his desk and stared at the screen, watching the emails stack up before his big black eyes.

At first we took pity on him and showed him how to respond. We even finished and sent off a few of his emails for him. All the same, with the best will in the world, we couldn't carry him for ever. Sooner or later, everyone has to stand on their own four feet and take responsibility. And the truth is, Freddie couldn't. He never seemed to learn, however many times we showed him. He just sat there with a bewildered look on his face.

At last matters came to a head, the day we got a furious complaint from one of our clients. It seems that on this occasion Freddie had, for a wonder, succeeded in sending an email. But as it only said something like '*ccvnbxxbnhfgc*' he might as well not have bothered. After the client had stormed in and stormed off, Boss Sally called Freddie to her office. She shut the door after him, but we could hear her voice raised in anger. 'Bad Freddie,' we heard. '*Bad* Freddie.'

There was a pause, then the door opened and he came out. We didn't dare raise our heads, but we could hear him as he trotted between the desks and left the office without a word. The place hasn't been quite the same since. I sometimes wonder what became of him.

THE OAK SPRITE

COUPLE OF DAYS BACK – I think it was Monday – we were down in the living room, which looks out on the back garden, and Julie said, 'Do you think that tree blocks the sunlight?'

'What tree?' I said.

'The tree in the back garden,' she said.

I looked out of the window. 'I suppose so,' I said, 'yes.'

So then she said maybe we should get it cut down. We'd get more sunlight, she said, and I could see the logic, so I said yes.

Then, later that night, Julie had gone to bed, and I was about to follow when I got a shock. I jumped. Because, you see, there was this knocking at the door – the back door, I mean. And that's odd, because the back door doesn't lead through to the front, it just goes into the back garden, and the back garden has a locked gate. So who it could be was more than I could think.

Anyway, I went to the back door and I opened it, and of course there wasn't anyone there. And I was just going to shut the door again when it was as if there was a voice.

'Excuse me,' it said.

And I opened the door again and looked out. There was still no one there – but then there was the voice again:

'Don't kill the oak.'

I looked out into the darkness and said, 'Hello?' – a bit cautiously, you know.

'Not you!' the voice said – which I didn't understand at all.

'Who's there?' I said; but the voice didn't answer, it just said: 'Every living thing is possessed by a sprite.'

I thought about that for a moment, and then I said something – I think it was, 'Oh.'

The voice went on. 'Kill the oak and you kill me.'

By now I was thoroughly confused by the whole business – there was a voice, but no one was there – and it wasn't making any sense. So I just said, 'I'm sorry.'

'I'm not talking to you,' it said.

So I asked again, 'What do you mean?'

But it just said again, 'Every living thing is possessed by a spirit,' which didn't take things any further. Then it said, 'Come outside. We must talk.'

And I almost stepped outside without thinking, but I stopped myself and I didn't. I looked out again into the dark night. And for a moment, something hung in the air. Then it was as if whatever it was had vanished.

I shut the door and, feeling a bit daft, went to bed.

Julie was asleep. The window was ajar, as she prefers. I lay in the dark waiting for sleep to come, and as I drifted off strange visions came to me on the wind that blew through the night.

Next morning at breakfast, Julie said she'd had a really weird dream, but she couldn't remember what it was, so that conversation didn't really go anywhere.

Then I went to work.

It was a quiet morning in the shop. A young couple, nice-looking, shy, came in mid-morning and asked about one of the phones.

I said, 'It comes with the latest version of Android and automatic security updates. It has free unlimited high-quality photo storage and a picture-in-picture mode' – I showed them that – 'and it lets you open an app while another one is still running. It's robust and shock-resistant and it's designed to withstand blows of tremendous force.' I keep a metal ruler on my desk, so I picked that up and hit the phone with it two or three times till the screen cracked. It was still lit up, and I showed it to them. 'You see,' I said. Then I dropped it on the tiled floor and stamped on it four or five times. The case smashed and the innards sprang out. 'Unfortunately this is a defective item, but,' I said, picking up the next phone from the display, 'you'll be absolutely delighted by the structural damage this little baby can experience.' I hurled it against the wall, where it broke open.

I could see the manager coming towards me, so I picked up the next two phones at the same time, using one to smash against the other in a repeated movement.

He tried to pull the phones out of my hands, but I wasn't having any of that, and he wasn't strong enough to stop me. The other assistants were stood there watching, but the manager shouted at them to help, and then one of the bigger guys came over and hit me in the mouth.

Five minutes later I was standing outside on the pavement. I walked around town till my feet got tired, then I sat on a bench. It was a warm day, and it was nice to watch the world go by.

At about one o'clock, I went home. I wanted some time to myself so I could work out what to say to Julie when she got back from the office.

But actually, when I let myself in, she was there already.

'Hello,' I said. 'You're home early.'

'I've got the sack,' she said.

'Now there's a coincidence,' I said.

And then she explained. 'Something came over me. I called my boss a fart-faced git. I said she was a fucking waste of space and a liability to Western civilisation. I said I'd picked more intelligent forms of life out of my nose. I said some other things too, which I've forgotten. Then she said, "Right, get out." So I did.'

Julie sat down opposite me, and she looked a bit shell-shocked – as if she was puzzled about what she'd done. So while I had the chance I told her what I'd done.

'What a shitshow,' she said.

We opened a bottle of wine and got smashed. It doesn't take much.

Then it was a bit later and we were talking it over, and I don't remember how we got on to it, but I said, 'It's all the sprite's fault.'

Well, Julie looked at me as if I was mad or something.

'What?' she said.

So I said it again. 'It's all the sprite's fault.'

But I could see she was still a bit confused, so I explained how the oak sprite had knocked at the back door and said 'Don't kill the oak' and 'everything's possessed by a spirit'.

An expression came across Julie's face like a smile, but a bit worried-looking too.

'Right,' she said. 'Possessed by a spirit.'

'Yes,' I said.

Then she came to a conclusion. 'You're pissed,' she said. 'As pissed,' she specified, 'as a fart.'

'Well, yes,' I said.

'Besides,' she said, 'it's not an oak, it's a beech.'

'What?' I said.

'It's not an oak tree, you dumbbell, it's a beech,' she said.

Then in that moment it all became clear to me.

'It's all clear to me,' I said, and I explained, 'This is what's been happening – I can see it all. The spirit of the oak, or the beech, or whatever: it's under threat. It knows we want to cut the tree down. And I mean, let's be fair, it's not going to be happy about that, is it? That's where it lives. So it came to stop us chopping the tree down. It got into us. Like you said, something came over us. It was the oak sprite, Julie. The oak sprite made us do it all.'

But then Julie shook her head. 'No,' she said. 'No. Look. You're saying this sprite...

Jesus… OK, this *sprite* came to you and said every living thing is possessed by a spirit. Yes?'

'Yes,' I said.

'And then it said it wasn't talking to you.'

I said yes again.

'It was telling you, only you were too thick to notice, it was *saying* that you have a sprite in *you*. Because, according to it, everyone does. It didn't want to speak to you, it wanted to talk to the sprite that's *in* you.'

I thought about this. 'I see,' I said.

She stood up. 'Come on,' she said. 'We're both very drunk − you've got me saying stuff that makes literally no sense, and now we've got to go into the back garden and talk to a tree.'

It was dark in the garden, but not cold. Soon we were stood in front of the tree. There was a dry, gentle breath of wind.

'Right,' said Julie loudly. She paused, uncertain. The tree remained a tree.

'Sprite,' she said, and we both felt very foolish. There was a pause, then I turned to go back in, and at the same time the voice spoke:

'Yes.'

It was like a bolt of electricity. I span round and looked at Julie. Had she heard it? Her eyes were full of shock. She nodded at me.

She's bolder than me. 'Who are you?' she said loudly.

And the voice came: 'You know who I am. I am the spirit of the oak.'

'It's a beech,' she said.

'What?' the sprite said.

'Look at the bloody leaves,' Julie said. 'It's not an oak, it's a beech.' Then she drew breath and went on: 'Anyway, you sprite. I hope you're bloody proud of yourself.'

'Sorry?'

'Yeah, so you should be. You came to us, didn't you, and you had a good old chat with the spirits that are in us and they... they cocked it up for both of us. Lost us our jobs, our livelihoods. So, mission accomplished. Well done. I mean – and I'm going to spell it out for you, because I don't know how familiar you are with sarcasm – what you have done is fucking *ruin* us. No jobs, no money. And without money we *die*. Do you hear me? While you're wafting about being all fey and folk cultural, we will be dying in a *ditch*.'

Julie can be very eloquent sometimes.

At length, the sprite's voice came, and it just said: 'Oh.'

And then: 'Well, I'm sorry about that. But you've got it wrong. Every living thing has a sprite. Of course it does. The spirit is what gives consciousness, it is the spark of magic. The spirit is you.'

And I said, 'What?'

And it said: 'I didn't want to talk to you, I didn't want to talk to the sprite. Why should I? We sprites, we cling to the branches, we're not at the root. I had to speak with the ape, the essence, the part buried deep. I thought if I could bring that to the surface, just a little bit, then maybe you – it, you – wouldn't want to kill the tree after all, and I would be saved. I'm sorry. It seemed the best way.'

We stood there for a while, not speaking.

'Who am I?' I thought. Is it true that I'm not the same thing all through? Am I – I mean, the real me – just the bit on the surface, the half-trained driver of an unruly engine? Then I thought about all the strange things I've done in my life without knowing why. The night seemed darker; the world seemed far away – even Julie.

Then the voice said: 'I can help you. It can make it all right again. It's really very easy. All you have to do is say yes.'

Suddenly, and the voice didn't even have to explain it, I saw exactly how it would be. Somehow, it didn't matter how, everything would go back to how it was. It would be as if what had happened hadn't. We'd have our jobs back, *and* our precious money; I would never have smashed those phones; Julie would never have called her boss a fart-faced git. Our futures would be *safe*.

It was a moment of decision. I looked at Julie, and I knew my answer.

'No,' I said. 'Thanks, but no.'

And Julie smiled and took my hand, and we walked back into the house, our futures gloriously unknown.

TROLL

HIS IS A STORY about Troll.

Don't ask me to describe Troll. Troll was a massive thing, and at the same time too small to be seen. Troll was great and dark and heavy and also a wisp in the wind. Troll was heavy and lumpen, and yet Troll faded away as soon as an eye was laid upon Troll. No one knew Troll. This was partly because of Troll's tricky presence, which I have described, but also because there were things about Troll that people did not want to know. Troll was certainly a monster. Troll had teeth that could bite a man in two and eyes that could burn a forest into stubble and great claws that could crush a house. These are some of the things that people did not want to know about Troll, and for this reason people did not know Troll. And so it was that Troll was quite alone.

Troll wanted to learn how to be seen, because Troll wanted to know how to make friends, but whatever Troll did no one could see Troll. So Troll followed a man through the streets. The man did not see Troll walking alongside him or standing in his shadow or flying overhead. Sometimes the man would pause in puzzlement and turn, but in that moment Troll would disappear by stepping behind a doorway or under a leaf.

The man stopped at a door and unlocked it and entered a house. Troll stepped in behind him so as not to be noticed. The man locked the door and boiled some water in a kettle, and then he poured the water into a mug which had a teabag in it. The man prepared his tea, and he went over to the sofa and sat down and checked his phone.

Troll stood in a dark corner watching the man. After a while Troll stepped closer to the sofa and sat down next to the man.

The man felt a presence without knowing why, and glanced to his side, but Troll hid behind the cushion and the man returned to his phone.

Throughout the day Troll watched the man going about his business. Troll wanted to know how people make friends, but the man did not seem to be making friends that day, so Troll did not learn. The man pottered about the house and checked his phone and read some pages from a book and made a meal on the stove, and then he ate the meal while listening to some music.

Several times Troll almost spoke to the man, and at other moments Troll almost decided not to hide when the man looked in Troll's direction. But Troll could not speak to the man, and could not even stay in sight when the man looked in Troll's direction. This made Troll very angry, because Troll was not able to do what Troll wanted to do, and the reason Troll could not do this was Troll.

The day darkened towards night. The man cooked himself his evening meal, which he ate in front of the television. He watched the screen for a long while, and then he washed his face and brushed his teeth and took off his clothes and went to bed. He picked up a book and read it for a little while.

Troll watched all this from behind the door and under the sofa and deep in the corner of the room. Troll was so sad that Troll almost howled. Even here in the man's house Troll was lonely, and there was nothing to be done.

Finally the man put the book to one side and snuggled down in bed and switched off the light.

'Good night, Troll,' the man said.

And all at once in the darkness of the room Troll was happy.

THE LIGHT BRIGADE

(RE-CHARGED)

ADAPTED FROM ALFRED,

LORD TENNYSON

Half a league, half a league,
    Half a league onward,
All in the valley of Death
    Rode the six hundred.
'Forward, the Light Brigade!
Charge for the guns!' he said.
'Which guns?'
        No sound he made,
But pointed the wrong way, the
    Stupid old dunderhead.
So to the valley of Death
    Rode the six hundred.

'Forward, the Light Brigade!'
Was there no man dismay'd,
When ev'ry soldier knew
    Someone had blunder'd?
Theirs was to make reply,
Theirs was to reason why,
Not just to do and die,
    Docile six hundred!
Still, to the valley of Death
    Rode the six hundred.

Cannon to right of them,
Cannon to left of them,
Cannon in front of them
    Volley'd and thunder'd;
Storm'd at with shot and shell,
Madly they rode pell-mell.
Into the jaws of Death,
Into the mouth of Hell
    Rode the six hundred.

Unsheathed their sabres bare,
Muscle and flesh to tear,
Hacking the gunners there,
Charging an army, while
    All the world wonder'd:

Ploughed through the battery-smoke,
Right through the line they broke;
Cossack and Russian
Kill'd by the sabre-stroke
    Shatter'd and sunder'd.
Kill them! Kill all you can!
Slaughter each horse and man,
    Manic six hundred!
Dodg'd they the shell and shot,
Tasted the blood and snot,
Kill'd and rode back, but not,
    Not the six hundred.

Corpses to right of them,
Corpses to left of them,
Corpses right under them
    Gutted and sunder'd;
Riddled by shot and shell,
Both horse and hero fell,
Gored and dismember'd well,
Crunch'd in the jaws of Death,
Chew'd in the mouth of Hell,
Till they who still had breath
    Saw it and chunder'd,
All that was left of them,
    Left of six hundred.

When will the madness fade?
O the wild charge they made!
　　All the world wonder'd.
Grieve for the charge they made!
Grieve for the Light Brigade,
　　Crazy six hundred!

JASPER

HILE WE WERE AWAY, we left Jasper, our Jack Russell terrier, with Uncle Henry. We flew back on Sunday night, slumped into bed and slept for twelve hours. We didn't feel up to going round and collecting him until the following afternoon.

When we arrived, Uncle Henry was out in the garden, shovelling the last of a pile of soil into a hole.

'Offal,' he said. 'How was Florida?'

'Lovely,' I said. 'I hope Jasper has been behaving himself?'

'Oh, he's been no trouble,' said Uncle Henry.

'Where is he?' I asked.

'Do come in and have a drink,' said Uncle Henry.

I looked round as we went in, but I couldn't see Jasper. 'Is he having a nap?' I asked.

'Tea, coffee? Something stronger?' Uncle Henry asked.

'Coffee, please,' I said. 'No milk or sugar.'

Linda wanted tea. We sat down. We talked about our holiday for a bit, and Uncle Henry admired our tans. He told us the latest news from the Rotary Club. At last, we got up to leave.

'Anyway,' I said, 'we'd better disturb Jasper and let him know we're back.'

'Pish and tush,' said Uncle Henry. 'You can pop in and collect him any time you like.'

'I'd like to have him now,' Linda said. 'We've missed him.'

'Tell you what,' said Uncle Henry, 'sit yourselves back down and I'll get you another drink. Whisky and splash?'

'Yes, but—'

'I insist.'

So we sat down again and he went over to the cabinet and measured out a generous portion for me.

'I'm driving,' said Linda. 'Just water.'

Uncle Henry got Linda some water and handed us our drinks.

'Jasper is... chin-chin' – he raised his glass – 'a lovely little dog. An absolute corker.'

'Thanks,' I said, taking a sip.

'He's just a bit under the weather, that's all. Nothing to signify. He'll be right as rain again in no time.'

Linda set down her water and looked at Uncle Henry. 'Where is he? What have you done with him?'

Uncle Henry raised a hand. 'There's really no need to worry,' he said. 'The vet's just giving him a once-over. He'll be back before you've noticed he's gone.'

'But,' Linda said, 'we *have* noticed he's gone.'

'Ha ha,' said Uncle Henry.

Linda stood up. 'Come on,' she said. 'Yes, you too, Uncle Henry.'

'Me?' said Uncle Henry.

'You,' said Linda, 'are taking us to the vets.'

We went in our car. The journey was a bit tense, but Uncle Henry kept things jolly. 'Jasper's a perky little beggar, isn't he?' he said. 'Many's the time he's nipped at my ankles. Bless his little cotton socks. Now I mind the time—'

'Shut up,' said Linda.

'My, my,' said Uncle Henry, giving me a glance.

Uncle Henry directed us there, and we parked up and went in to reception. He strode up to the desk, bared his teeth and said: 'Ah, young lady, we'd like to see the vet, please.'

The receptionist looked at him without smiling. 'Do you have an appointment?' she asked.

'No, we do not. You see—' Uncle Henry began.

'What's it about?'

'Jasper.'

'You what?' she asked.

'It's about Jasper, our dog,' Linda said.

'Jack Russell,' I said.

'Jack, as my nephew so rightly says, Russell,' Uncle Henry said. 'You will recall I brought the little fellow in earlier as he was feeling a wee bit on the peaky side, and I was worried. You remember?'

'No.'

'Well, well, you see a lot of people. Anyway, if we might just, you know, toddle on through and see how little Jasper is getting on, then—'

'We don't have no Jack Russells here,' said the receptionist.

'Oh, piffle, of course you do. I brought him in myself this morning. Now I'm sure if you will just take a look at that absolutely tip-top database of yours—'

She stood up without a word and walked away behind the scenes.

'Courtesy,' Uncle Henry muttered in my direction, 'is dead.'

Five minutes later, she came back. 'I told you,' she said. 'We don't have no Jack Russells. You must've been mistaken.'

'Madam,' said Uncle Henry, 'I am never mistaken. Check again.'

'We haven't got none,' she said.

Next, the vet came out. 'What's the problem?' she asked.

We explained what the problem was.

'I spoke to you about it this morning,' said Uncle Henry.

'No, you didn't,' said the vet. 'I've never seen you before in my life.'

'But this is absurd,' said Uncle Henry. 'I was here this morning. I saw you about Jasper, just as plain as I'm standing here.'

'No, you didn't. I wasn't even in this morning.'

Uncle Henry looked at them both with a magnificent disdain. 'I have but one word for you, and that is tosh and balderdash. However, if you are going to maintain this unhelpful attitude, there is clearly no point in our pursuing the discussion. Come.' He swept out of the surgery, Linda and I following in his wake. The vet and the receptionist stared after us.

Back in the car, Linda asked: 'What have you done with him?'

'I told you,' said Uncle Henry. 'Jasper is being looked after by the veterinarians. I can't conceive why they are being so awkward about it.'

'This is ridiculous! Of course they don't have him,' said Linda.

'Yes they do,' said Uncle Henry. 'I brought him here myself.'

'They said they don't, Henry. They said it just now,' said Linda.

'Oh, don't take any notice of that. They'll come round.'

'What?' I asked.

'It's just their way. Now don't you distress yourself over this absurd business one second longer. Leave it all to your Uncle Henry.'

'Henry,' Linda said, 'Jasper wasn't there. He just wasn't.'

Uncle Henry looked over at Linda for a while. 'Well,' he said, finally. 'Well. I must say I am surprised and a little wounded to see you taking their word over that of your own flesh and blood. However, I am big enough to rise above the slings and arrows. I'll tell you what we'll do. We'll wait till you've calmed down, and then we'll sort it all out. Tomorrow.'

So we left it at that.

Linda drove us back to Uncle Henry's place.

'You must stay for dinner,' said Uncle Henry. 'It's the least I can do.'

'Yes,' Linda said, 'it is.'

As soon as we entered the house, Uncle Henry went into the kitchen and shut the door in our faces. 'Don't come in,' he called out to us. 'I absolutely forbid you. This is my special treat. My pièce de résistance.' So we stayed in the living room, talking in undertones.

We heard from the kitchen the loud slams of a meat cleaver on a chopping board and the rending of flesh. At intervals, the sounds would cease, and Henry would burst in, his apron smeared with blood, to top up our glasses with some choice wine.

At first, we chatted brightly and without cessation, Linda and I. Then, little by little, imperceptibly, pausing more, thinking more, at last we stopped talking, and the silence descended, and we sat, our glasses empty, awaiting the awful moment when Uncle Henry would appear at the door, and announce that dinner was served.

THE

SEIZED MOMENT

‘ AKE! Aren't you ready yet? We're going!'

'I'm coming!' Jake called down from his room.

'Come on, then!'

Jake did not really want to go on the demonstration. Fourteen years of age, he had better things to do with his time on a Saturday morning. However, he knew he ought to show willing. After all, as Jake's mum said, 'You want to be able to say you were part of the resistance.'

Before they left the house, Jake was able to slip a bottle of hand sanitiser into a coat pocket and a battered copy of *Eggs, Beans and Crumpets* into another.

He got in the car. He had to hunch himself in the corner of the back seat to leave room for the placards.

'Where are we going?' he asked once they had set off.

'Jake!' said Jake's dad. 'We've told you a thousand times.'

It turned out that the demonstration was in Eckersdyke Market Square, twenty miles away. The demonstration had been announced on Facebook last night by a Dark Resistance group. Jake's dad had been all over it at once. 'This is our chance to make a difference!' he had said.

It was a sunny but blustery spring morning somewhere near the end of the first lock-down. Jake watched the empty streets as they rolled by.

'That's one good thing about the Fake Virus,' Jake's dad said. 'No traffic to speak of. We should have a clear run all the way.' He drove on a little while, then he said, 'Sheep!'

'Where?' said Jake's mum.

'I mean people,' said Jake's dad. 'Locking themselves up in their homes on a lovely day like this, just because they've been told to. Sheep.'

'Oh, yes,' said Jake's mum.

Jake watched the clouds as they sped across the blueness above. The trees were full and shaking. A bird – he did not know its name – swept across his line of sight in an impossible arc.

'Oh,' said Jake's mum. 'There's a mast over there.'

'Yes,' said Jake's dad.

'Be careful,' said Jake's mum.

'Poor bastards – mind my French,' said Jake's dad. 'I mean the folks who have to live round here with that thing stuck up their nose without so much as a by-your-leave. Everyone knows what masts do to your electrons, but no one will stand up and say it. But don't worry, we'll be fine. It's only a few seconds. There, we're past it already.'

'Are you sure?' said Jake's mum.

'We're fine,' said Jake's dad.

They arrived in Eckersdyke shortly before the demonstration. They found a parking space a little way from the market square.

Jake's dad unloaded the placards from the back of the car, and they took one each. Jake's dad had 'DON'T LIE! WE WON'T DIE!' which was a reference to the Fake Virus, and Jake's mum was reusing an old one that said 'GIVE US A SOVEREIGN!', an allusion to national sovereignty which, as far as Jake could tell, no one understood without it being explained to them in some detail. Jake's sign said 'I WANT A FUTURE' without an exclamation mark. His parents considered it rather a vague request in comparison to their own, and somewhat lacking in punch, but perhaps for that reason they passed it for his use.

They put on their masks before walking to the square. There had been some debate about this. Jake's dad had said they shouldn't wear masks, because masks were a symbol of the Deep State Conspiracy to suppress the People. Jake's mum had said yes, that was true, but on the other hand wearing a mask would make it more difficult for the Deep State Conspiracy to track them down if they happened to be watching. There followed a number of statements, all starting with 'Yes, but'. In the end, it was Jake's mum's view that prevailed, to Jake's relief.

Others joined them as they walked down the street. Most were not wearing masks, and Jake's parents, seeing this, removed theirs. No one took any great care to keep socially distant. These people seemed to conform to a definite type: the same type as Jake's parents. First they were few; then they numbered dozens, and more appeared from side streets as they went, walking close. Jake felt himself tensing. It had been a long time since he had stood alongside so many people.

And then they were standing at the mouth of a short street leading down an incline into the square. The square was a sea of pink faces. The air was filled with the low growl of their talk.

The moment hit Jake like a blow. He had intended to maintain a detached attitude throughout, but now he saw he could not. He stopped in his tracks and he could not move. His parents, not noticing him, walked straight into the sea. The alarms in his head which he had shut out and ignored rang loud and brazen and beat him down. His mouth was dry and he could not swallow and he forgot to breathe and his heart raced and he felt both flushed and pale and he wondered if he was going to vomit and he shut his eyes and the sounds roared and he wanted to turn and run and he was afraid the crowd would trample him over and he staggered to the side of the street and no one could see him and he gasped for breath as the world buzzed.

Slowly, he returned to himself.

His parents had disappeared. That made his next move easier. He turned back and walked away from the square. There were more pouring down the street, but he almost pressed himself against the wall and he was able to maintain a distance.

Without having made any decision, he was heading back to the car. He found himself observing his own actions with a kind of unconcerned curiosity. The world around him was remote but vivid: the buildings seemed harder and solider than before, the breeze breezier, the trees more treelike.

He was back at the car now. It was locked, of course. He saw a green bench a short way further down the street, and he made his way towards it. The bench did not seem to be much used, and he sat carefully, not touching it with his hands. He propped his placard against the side of the bench. It was a quiet spot a little way from the square. There was a tree just behind him which leant out over the railing of a small park and extended a shivering canopy of leaves over him.

His phone buzzed in his pocket. He ignored it.

After a while, he stopped staring across the street at an empty shop, which was what he discovered he had been doing. He used his hand sanitiser, then he reached into his other pocket and took out his book. Soon he was reading.

His phone buzzed again, but it stopped after a while.

He did not know how long it was before his parents came back. It may have been an hour.

'Jake!'

Jake looked up.

'Hello,' he said.

'Where have you been!' Jake's mum said. Jake didn't think this required an answer, so he stayed quiet. She continued: 'We've been worried sick! We rang you!'

'You missed a treat,' said Jake's dad. 'Timmy Tomkins was there, and he gave a speech. It was very inspiring. He made everything clear.'

On the way back home, his parents told him all about the demonstration. They had been able to trade ideas with the like-minded about the Fake Virus, phone masts, chemtrails, metropolitan elites, the Woke Brigade, Remoaners, Sheeple, Illegals, the BBC, the NHS, and so on and so forth. They had had such a good time that they even forgave Jake for sneaking off.

'It's your loss,' said Jake's dad. 'When you look back, you'll see. You could have made a difference. You can't be a sheep all your life, Jake. You've got to seize the moment. You've got to stand up for what you believe in.'

'Yes, Dad,' said Jake.

INSIDE STORY

I

O, I'M VERY HAPPY here. The chains hardly incommode me at all. They're a bit uncomfortable, perhaps, but what do you expect? Compared to other people, I'm very lucky.

It's dark, but that only means the light doesn't hurt my eyes. I can see everything I need.

The walls are made of stone. The stone is damp, and each block is curved and worn. There is a sort of slimy green growth on it in patches.

There is a grille in the wall at the far end, two bars vertical and two horizontal. Sometimes light comes through it, if the sun is in the right place.

A man visits me occasionally. I don't know his name. He doesn't speak to me; he just leaves food and drink.

II

Today I realised the chains are loose. I can loosen them at my wrists to restore the circulation. I don't remember them being so loose before.

In fact, they are almost dropping off my arms. I'll have to be careful they don't fall off accidentally.

III

This morning the man came in, and he stopped in surprise. 'Are you still here?' he said.

'Yes,' I said. It was the first time I had spoken in I don't know how long. My voice came out all croaky.

'Don't you want to go?' he said.

'What?' I said.

He repeated what he had said.

'Where would I go?' I asked.

'That's none of my business,' he said.

'But I'm a prisoner,' I said.

He came over to me and pulled the chains off my wrists.

'The door is open,' he said.

'What are you saying?' I said.

He sighed. 'Just go, will you?'

'Why? Don't you want me here?'

'I'm sorry. We just can't afford you any more.'

Then he let me out.

IV

The world is a great shock to me. The sky is too high; there could be anything there. The spaces are too big. The air moves. Everything is dangerous.

I pressed myself back against the wall.

'You can't stay here,' he said.

'Why not?' I said. 'I've left, haven't I? I'm outside, am I not?'

He shrugged. 'Suit yourself,' he said, and went back in.

I sat down against the wall and watched the world go by. After a while, it stopped spinning.

People walked past. They seemed oblivious to the danger. Couldn't they see there was no roof?

The wall was solid against my back. I could press my hands against the ground. The ground was reassuringly hard. There were bits of gravel that dug into my palms. The pain was a great comfort to me.

I found it helped to shut my eyes. I could pretend I was still inside.

'Hello?'

The voice was unexpected. I opened my eyes. There was a man crouching in front of me.

'Hello,' I said.

'Are you all right?' he said.

'Yes, go away,' I said.

'Are you sure?'

'Yes.'

He went away.

V

The street was quieter now. The light faded until it was almost as dark as the prison – or it would have been, except that the street lights flicked on when the darkness came. Still, when that happened it did mean I couldn't see the sky, and I could pretend the lights were in a ceiling.

I stood up and took a few steps down the street, pressing my hand against the wall. My breath came quick; I couldn't get enough air in my lungs.

I came to the corner of the street, and I paused, unable to go a step further.

Then the man was standing in front of me again.

'Are you sure I can't help you?' he said.

'Oh,' I said. 'Yes, please help me.'

He bought me a bacon roll and a cup of coffee at a café. 'Thank you,' I said. 'You're very kind.'

'Have you anywhere to stay?' he asked.

VI

So he brought me to this place. I don't know how long I've been here. It's very nice.

He locks me in and I don't have to leave the house.

He says he's going to find me some chains next week.

A CHANGE IN

THE AIR

HE PALACE of Westminster, that gaudy cathedral of politics, shone absurdly in the morning sun. In its shadow, Parliament Square held a shop-soiled promise of spring. And in the square there stood, as usual, the surly double-sized figure of Churchill, cast in black bronze, clad in a long greatcoat, the stick in its right hand planted firmly into its tall plinth, its left foot pressed forward, its broad back crooked with the weight of history, its squat face staring with grim resolution towards the high clock tower of Big Ben.

No one knows for sure why the statue of Churchill came to life that morning. There was no thunderbolt, no mystic incantation, just a faint shudder across its frame and a slow movement of its head. Some say they felt a change in the air, a north wind that became westerly; and if that does not seem explanation enough, maybe there is no other.

For a long while nothing further happened, though what had been dead was now living. Then, with a deep sigh, the statue of Churchill moved.

The statue flicked its eyes to left and right. It advanced cautiously to the edge of the plinth and assessed the nine-foot drop. It crouched down slowly until it was sitting with its hollow legs dangling over the edge, and pushed itself forward and dropped to the ground with a clang.

By this time, a small crowd had gathered at a short distance and was looking on in silent astonishment. The statue, oblivious, stooped and felt the grass at its feet, and made a sound from within – not a word, but a soft sigh, hollow and resonant and somehow melancholy. It sat on the grass, its legs drawn up and its head down, staring with wonder at the green blades between its fingers.

A small dog of indeterminate breed wandered up to it, and before the man at the other end of its lead could react the dog cocked its leg and marked the statue. The onlookers gave out an involuntary 'Oh' and held their breath. The statue reached out a hand to the dog and tenderly stroked its fur for a few seconds. The dog enjoyed the attention for as long as it lasted and then trotted, unconcerned, back to the man holding the lead.

The incident seemed to be a signal for everyone to relax and accept that the statue meant them no harm. In no time they were greeting it like an old friend, and it smiled and nodded at them with perfect patience and amiability.

Word was getting out. News teams were alerted and were on their way to the scene as fast as their vans would take them. It was the Prime Minister who heard of the matter next; only a minute or two had passed and already he could be observed strolling nonchalantly across New Palace Yard towards the great bronze figure, which was still seated on the grass and allowing two boisterous children of a young family to climb over it and even to stroke its bald head.

The Prime Minister approached the group; the family were quick to take fright and retreat. For a moment, the statue looked at him. The Prime Minister spoke, and gestured towards his media team, who were running towards them with their cameras jangling. The statue's face shut down. It spoke: a soft, wordless sigh. The Prime Minister smiled and nodded. The statue tried again: this time, a deep, mournful groan emerged. It shook its head, without preamble reached out and grasped the Prime Minister by the waist, stood up, elevating the Prime Minister above its shoulders at the same time, swung him round and placed him without fuss on the tall ledge of the plinth. It turned, took up its stick from the earth, into which it had been thrust, and stumped off. Behind it, the Prime Minister's cries faded into the distance. 'Hello! Just one photo? Shaking hands?… Could you get me down please? Hello?'

Many stories are told of what the statue did next, though not all can be given credence. It's said that the statue foiled a mugging, punched a racist, saved a cat, joined a protest march, spoke with the King. Some swear it went down to the Embankment and made fast friends with the homeless there, that it stormed into Westminster Abbey and smashed the tills, taking the spoils out to the waiting crowd of vagrants. The details of such tales will not stand much scrutiny. It was a time of rumour and speculation. The camera crews, arriving too late to capture the statue on film, were reduced to garnering expert opinion from across the board. Churchill specialists spoke of the great man's oratory and his place in history, of his eccentricities and his humour, of his bigotry and his racism. They reminded viewers of the protests the statue had attracted over the years: the paint thrown over it, the modifications made to its hairstyle, the slogans daubed across its plinth, the barriers put up for its protection. A classicist talked of the legend of Pygmalion. A folklorist spoke of King Arthur's promised return from the grave at time of need. Another, whose name we do not recall, said: 'Let's be clear. This is not Churchill; Churchill is dead and gone to his honoured grave. Whatever this thing is, it is not the man whose virtues and vices we rake over with such glee. It is the statue of Churchill made by Ivor Roberts-Jones. Many of us have passed by him every day for as long as we remember. There he stands on his pedestal, so that we all look up to him literally, and he scowls back down at us and our puny follies. We invest this idol of Churchill with our hopes and dreams… perhaps all these wishes and dreams were somehow received by him – I mean his statue – and maybe they built up over time until, at last, they give to him a kind of *life*… If that's the case, don't expect this Churchill to be like the Churchill that lived. Expect instead the person we want him to be, the person we want to be ourselves. Wouldn't that be nice? Anyway, here's how to make roulade.'

Later, as the day waned towards dusk, the statue sat on the Embankment wall, gazing over the murky waters of the Thames. By its side, also staring out over the great river, sat a figure less than half its size, a shaggy-haired, dirty-nailed man clad in layers of woollens.

'What a day, eh!' the man said. 'A day to be marked. They won't forget this day. They'd better not.'

A tourist boat chugged past. The passengers waved and cheered at the statue, and the statue and the man waved back.

'They love you,' the man said. 'Of course they do.'

The sky was changing minute by minute; slate became a darkening blue. The man sighed.

'Time's nearly up – you'll have to be getting back to your pedestal.'

The noise that came from the statue was almost a howl. The man looked into its face, which was momentarily contorted like a mask of pain. He stared for a long time.

'It's where you belong,' he said at last. 'Don't you want to be back on your pedestal? Well, maybe not. It must be lonely up there. But you can't stay down here, you know that. They would never stand for it. You cause too much trouble.'

He stopped himself.

'What am I saying? Why not cause them a bit of trouble – they cause us enough. And what are they going to do, arrest you? No, that wouldn't look good. They might try to make things hard for you, mind. But what can they do? They can't do anything.

'Look at that. Isn't that beautiful? Night-time. Bloody London. So much history you could chew it. But here and now… Jesus. What a mess. We've cocked it all up, haven't we? How can you save us when we can't even save ourselves? What a bloody mess. Too late now, I suppose. Maybe we'll do better next time.

'It's nice here. No, don't move. You're warm, do you know that? How can you be so warm? I'll stay here just a bit longer. Rest my eyes. I hope you don't mind. That's nice.'

When the man woke, it was morning and the statue was nowhere to be seen. He checked the plinth, but it was empty. He turned and walked towards Westminster Bridge. Outside a newsagent, a poster proclaimed the Prime Minister's resignation.

AND AFTERWARDS

HEN I STEPPED into the road, I was looking at my phone. It was a picture of a tree.

I felt a breath of wind and then all at once pain like I have never felt before, at the same time hearing a bang and shouting and then silence.

The tree is the last thing I saw.

The pain carried on for longer than I could take. Then it flamed so hard that my nerves burned out, one by one.

The pain faded.

I tried to move, but that made things worse, so I didn't.

Sometimes I thought I could hear things a very long way off, like voices, but as soon as I tried to listen they went away.

There were bits of sound and feeling, and even sight, I think, a colour, a dull red, maybe.

I was slowly floating away from myself.

Soon there was only a slow beat, a breathing in and out.

Then there wasn't.

My thoughts faded.

Time lost meaning.

I could feel when they moved me. They did it very carefully, almost tenderly. They put me in a case and made sure I was tidy. After a while they put a lid on the case. Then they picked up the case and, again very gently and slowly, as if I would break, they moved me to a place amongst trees and shrubs and they put me down again.

Then I feel the heaviness of earth above me.

I can feel the me that is me retreating, leaving my fingertips, my eyes, my ears. It isn't in my brain or my heart. It, me, I, go deeper, retreating like like like. I go deep and hide.

The flesh, the muscles and the fat, the intestines, the organs, the nerves and the bowels, the brain and heart, liver and kidneys decay. The cells soften and burst and mingle. The body sags.

There is a rustle too soft to be heard. A bug lands on my neck and finds nourishment. Soon it is inside me and still eating. More follow.

A small collapse. A scattering of dirt on my face, more on my body and legs. A crack, and more comes down. Now the earth presses hard.

I am a feast. Bugs and worms find me and invade. Roots probe and twine through me. They feed on me making an hour's life they take me off

now I am further within I have no flesh earth mud worms me we are one bones are me I am bones no thinking no breathing no feeling just me at rest for ever no hurt no harm to reach me within these bones no more to come nothing

above the tree blooms

and the life is never ending

HAPPY ENDING

N THE NICK OF TIME, they gained the courage to face the catastrophe that threatened their existence. Marshalling all their resources, they ruthlessly attacked the root of the problem. Having slain every last human, the bees lived happily ever after in the saved world.

DEBTS AND THANKS

If you've managed to read this far, I admire and esteem you for your tenacity, and you can stop now. Nothing from here on is of any interest. It's just thank-you speeches.

At the end of the *Canterbury Tales*, Geoffrey Chaucer wrote: 'if ther be any thyng that displese hem [the reader], I preye hem also that they arrette it to the defaute of myn unkonnynge, and nat to my wyl, that wolde ful fayn have seyd bettre if I hadde had konnynge.' Chaucer's meaning seems fairly clear, in spite of his frankly atrocious spelling, and I would like to claim a similar dispensation. I have tried to fill these stories of mine with signs and visions and, of course, jokes, and any failure on my part should, like his, be attributed to a lack of cunning, not of will.

Foremost among the folks I must thank is Will Dady, creator of Renard Press, who firstly said 'yes', and then guided this little book through to publication, giving the words a much-needed scrub and polish along the way.

I would also like to thank Suzanne, for more reasons than I can say here, but especially, in this context, for liking the kind of stories I write; Mum and Dad, for all their love and patience and making me who I am; and my brother Mark, just because.

I would like to thank Neil Gaiman and Chris Riddell for their book *Art Matters*, which gave me the encouragement I needed to write these stories.

I'd like to thank Claire Cronin of Loft Books, for publishing a version of 'The Oak Sprite' in Loft Books' *Anthology IV*. I wrote 'Happy Ending' as a tweet in 2019 in response to a daily Twitter challenge from the publisher Unbound: thank you. Many of the other stories in this book were written for publication in various literary magazines who, in the event, decided not to. The stories would not exist were it not for those magazines, and so, in all sincerity and with only the slightest tinge of wryness, I would like to thank them, too.

I'd like to thank Rose Drew and Alan Gillott of Stairwell Books for their encouragement and support in the making of my novel *Down to Earth*.

The ripples expand; the spheres of influence extend; the thanks multiply.

Over the years, many people have encouraged me in my writing. I remember Andrew Loretto and Matt Blackmore providing an invaluable and invigorating and slightly scary crash course in how to (re)write a play, a little more than twenty years ago. The lessons linger still. Jonathan Hall taught me more about drama and how to write it than can be said in these few lines. The late lamented Bradford University Theatre Group (BUTG), the still thriving Actors Community Theatre (ACT), and many others, have their place in my temples of gratitude. If yours is one of the many names I should have mentioned but have not, again, please blame my lack of cunning, not of will.

Others have helped to make me the writer of these stories, for good or ill, but without my ever meeting them. Robert Sheckley, Voltaire and Saki; W.S. Gilbert and P.G. Wodehouse; Terry Pratchett and Douglas Adams; Evelyn Waugh; G.K. Chesterton; Alan Plater and Preston Sturges, Agatha Christie and Dashiell Hammett; David Nobbs; Jonathan Coe; Flann O'Brien; Spike Milligan; H.G. Wells; Stella Gibbons; J.B. Priestley; Oscar Wilde; Samuel Beckett; N.F. Simpson; yes, and Geoffrey Chaucer too: a whole library of big books has helped to make this little one.

Well, as Wilde told us, all art is quite useless – this book perhaps more than most. Nevertheless, something inside us tells us to keep trying – to keep failing, but to keep trying – to send little messages to the present and the future in order to assure ourselves that, whatever has happened, we have not gone yet, and that whatever is to come, there is, while we can still send these messages, still hope.

ABOUT THE AUTHOR

ANDREW CROWTHER is not only the Secretary of the W.S. Gilbert Society, author of the major biography *Gilbert of Gilbert and Sullivan*, and the undisputed authority on the life and works of W.S. Gilbert, but is also himself a writer, author of the short novel *Down to Earth* and a variety of comic plays including *Welcome to Paradise*, *Funny Men* and *Working Lives*. His works seem to share with Gilbert's a heartfelt belief in the complete nonsensicality of the universe.

ANDREWCROWTHER.CO.UK

WWW.RENARDPRESS.COM

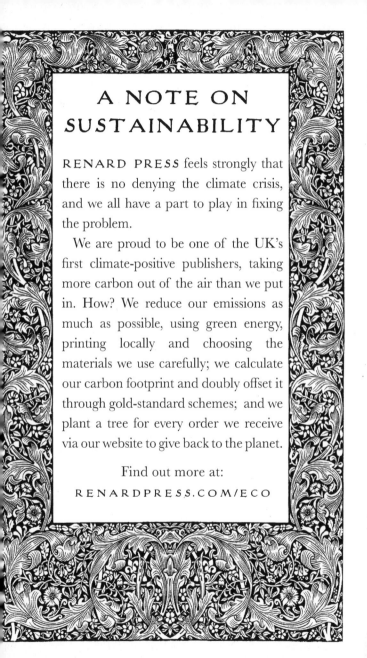

A NOTE ON SUSTAINABILITY

RENARD PRESS feels strongly that there is no denying the climate crisis, and we all have a part to play in fixing the problem.

We are proud to be one of the UK's first climate-positive publishers, taking more carbon out of the air than we put in. How? We reduce our emissions as much as possible, using green energy, printing locally and choosing the materials we use carefully; we calculate our carbon footprint and doubly offset it through gold-standard schemes; and we plant a tree for every order we receive via our website to give back to the planet.

Find out more at:

RENARDPRESS.COM/ECO

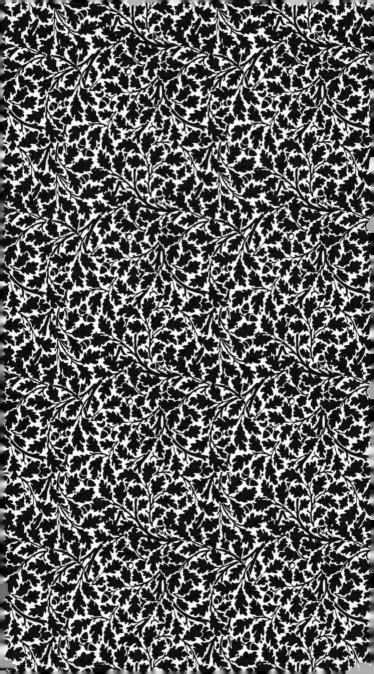